A Vision of Horror

The gentlemen hurried out of the courtyard without a word. It wasn't until they had reached the busy main street and were surrounded by the cheerful bustle of the crowds again that Mr. Utterson glanced at his friend's face. Mr. Enfield was pale and his eyes were filled with fear, as if he had just seen something too monstrous to speak of. Mr. Utterson knew his own face bore a look of answering fright. A look of sheer terror passed between them.

"God help the poor man," Mr. Utterson murmured.

READ ALL THE BOOKS
IN THE **WISHBONE** *classics* SERIES:

WISHBONE Classics

The Strange Case of
DR. JEKYLL & MR. HYDE

retold by Joanne Mattern

Interior illustrations by Ed Parker
Wishbone illustrations by
Kathryn Yingling

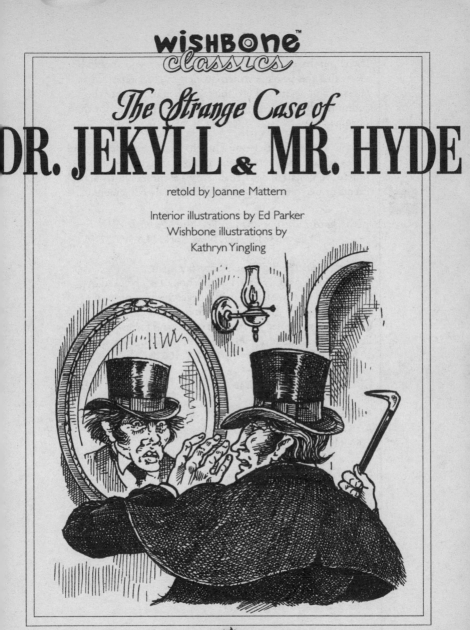

HarperPaperbacks
A Division of HarperCollinsPublishers

HarperPaperbacks *A Division of* HarperCollins*Publishers*
10 East 53rd Street, New York, N.Y. 10022

Cover photographs by Carol Kaelson

A Creative Media Applications Production
Art Direction by Fabia Wargin Design
Edited by Stacy Prince

First printing: October 1996

Printed in the United States of America

HarperPaperbacks and colophon are trademarks of
HarperCollins*Publishers*
WISHBONE is a trademark and service mark of
Big Feats! Entertainment

❖ 10 9 8 7 6 5 4 3 2 1

MR. G. J. UTTERSON

Introduction

All set to enter a world of action, adventure, drama, and laughs? Then come along with me, **Wishbone**. You may have seen me on my TV show. Often I am the main character and sometimes I am the sidekick, but I'm always right in the middle of a thrilling story. Now, I'm going to be your guide as we explore one of the world's greatest books — THE STRANGE CASE OF DR. JEKYLL AND MR. HYDE. Together we'll meet a lot of interesting characters and discover places we've never been! I guarantee lots of surprises too! So find a nice comfy chair, and get ready to read with **Wishbone**.

Table of Contents

Robert Louis Stevenson

Robert Louis Stevenson was born in Edinburgh, Scotland, on November 13, 1850. He was often sick as a child and had to spend a lot of time in bed. This gave him plenty of time to use his imagination. As he lay under the covers, Stevenson created stories about imaginary places and drew pictures of his make-believe worlds.

Stevenson's family wanted him to be an engineer like his father. Engineers use math and science to construct things such as bridges and buildings. But Stevenson did not like math and science. He wanted to be a writer.

Although he loved his family very much, by the time Stevenson was a young man, he was anxious to leave home and start his own life. Because he was sickly and weak, Stevenson's mother and father still treated him like a child. Finally Stevenson's doctor told his parents how unhappy their son was. His family agreed to let Stevenson leave home. Stevenson immediately set sail for France and began his career as a writer.

Over the next twenty years, Robert Louis Stevenson traveled to many places and wrote many exciting books. Some of his most popular works are *Treasure Island, Kidnapped, The Black Arrow*, and *The Strange Case of Dr. Jekyll and Mr. Hyde*.

Stevenson loved to travel. Nothing was more exciting to him than living in different places and seeing new things. One of the places Stevenson lived was the United States. Here he met and married an American woman named Fanny Osbourne, and became the stepfather of her children.

Stevenson and his family spent the last few years of his life living on the island of Samoa. Stevenson kept writing until his sudden death on December 3, 1894. He left behind a library of wonderful stories and adventures that readers still enjoy today.

ABOUT THE STRANGE CASE OF DR. JEKYLL AND MR. HYDE

I hate it when somebody yells at me and calls me a bad dog! I may get into trouble once in a while—okay, I get into trouble a lot. But I'm not a bad dog. Just like everyone else, I'm good sometimes and not so good other times. Each of us has a good side and a bad side. But what if there were a person who was completely bad? What would this person be like?

*T*he *Strange Case of Dr. Jekyll and Mr. Hyde* is the story of just such a person. Set in the city of London, England, this book tells the story of a well-known, respected London doctor named Henry Jekyll and a wicked man named Edward Hyde. The relationship between these two men is stranger than you think—and it forces everyone they know to confront their own feelings about good and evil.

The Strange Case of Dr. Jekyll and Mr. Hyde is set during the late 1800s, during a time known as the Victorian era. This time period was called

"Victorian" after Queen Victoria, who sat on the throne of England from 1837 to 1901. The Victorian era was a time of great change. New inventions were transforming the ways people worked and lived. People could travel from one city to another in just a few hours on a train, instead of spending several days bumping along in a horse-drawn carriage. Clothes were produced in large amounts by huge factories, rather than being sewn one at a time at home.

Despite the progress being made in travel, industry, and other areas, the people of the Victorian era were very old-fashioned. They followed strict rules regarding everything from what clothes they wore to how they held their teacups at dinner! Some of these rules seem ridiculous today, but they were taken very seriously by the Victorians. If a man showed up at a formal dance in casual clothes, not only would he be laughed at, he would probably lose his standing as an important person and be snubbed by all his friends.

The reason for all of these rules and regulations was that Victorians had a very strong sense of each person's place in society. If you were from a rich and important family, you were expected to grow up to be rich and important too. And rich and important people had to act in a certain way. A person's reputation—what people thought about him or her—was that person's most precious possession. But even if a person had a good reputation, he or she had to constantly live up to it. Anyone caught doing anything seriously wrong found that his or her reputation was ruined—forever. Once a person had a bad reputation, there was little chance for him or her to change and become well-respected. Today, if a person gets into trouble, that person is often given a second chance to change his or her ways. But there were no second chances in Victorian life.

These super-strict rules about good and bad behavior are a problem for Mr. Utterson, the main character of *The Strange Case of Dr. Jekyll and Mr. Hyde*. Several times in the story, he faces a terrible choice. Should he help his friend, Dr. Henry Jekyll, who is clearly in deep trouble, and risk ruining both of their reputations? Or should Mr. Utterson keep quiet to protect Dr. Jekyll, as well as his own public image as a man who can be trusted to keep a secret?

Dr. Jekyll also struggles to follow society's rules. He comes from a good family, and everyone thinks he is a fine, upstanding citizen. But it seems that Dr. Jekyll has done some very bad things. He knows that if anyone ever finds out about his behavior, his comfortable life and good reputation will be destroyed. And so Dr. Jekyll is forced to live a lie—and keep his dark deeds a secret.

During the 1800s, many important discoveries about science and medicine were being made. There was a great deal of interest in scientific explanations for every part of life. Because of the great changes science brought to their lives, the Victorians felt that anything was possible, if they could only learn enough. Robert Louis Stevenson was fascinated by the power of science, but this power also frightened him. He explores this fear in *The Strange Case of Dr. Jekyll and Mr. Hyde* as he shows the reader how science can even change the way a person thinks and acts.

This tale is a terrific mystery, full of excitement and puzzling events. Stevenson often sets the mood of his story through the setting—the foggy streets of London. You'll notice that many of the scariest moments in the story happen at night, when it is dark outside. Often, the characters find themselves alone on a deserted street, surrounded by a damp fog that chills the bones and makes everything look creepy and strange. Settings like this make the reader feel uneasy and nervous—and they tell us that something scary is about to happen.

I don't know about you, but all this talk has given me quite an appetite for this fascinating story! I can't wait another minute to find out what happens in this twisted tale! It's time to turn the page and take a tasty bite out of THE STRANGE CASE OF DR. JEKYLL AND MR. HYDE!

MAIN CHARACTERS

Gabriel John Utterson—a lawyer and friend of Dr. Jekyll

Richard Enfield—a friend of Mr. Utterson

Edward Hyde—an evil man

Dr. Henry Jekyll—a respected doctor

Dr. Hastie Lanyon—a friend of Dr. Jekyll and Mr. Utterson

Poole—Dr. Jekyll's butler

Sir Danvers Carew—a well-known London politician

Inspector Newcomen—a police officer

Mr. Guest—Mr. Utterson's friend and head clerk

1
The Mysterious Door

Our story begins one Sunday afternoon in the busy city of London. Two gentlemen are out for a walk. One is a lawyer named Mr. Gabriel John Utterson—a serious, calm, well-mannered man of about fifty years of age who is respected by the most important people in London.

Mr. Utterson is the type of fellow who is always happy to listen to someone's troubles and do his best to help the person out. His companion is his young friend, Mr. Richard Enfield, who loves to have a good time and is popular with everyone he meets. Although the two men have very different personalities, they are good friends and never miss their Sunday walk together.

Mr. Utterson and Mr. Enfield made their way down a quiet side street. This street was a sharp contrast to the rather gloomy, shabby neighborhood around it. All the houses were well-kept, with freshly painted shutters on the windows, polished brass knockers on the doors, and a clean, sparkling look to everything. The street was like a shiny jewel standing out from the dust.

But there was one building on the street that was not bright and cheerful. This sinister structure loomed over the street like a monster, with no windows to brighten the wall on that side—just a door on the first floor. This door had neither bell nor knocker, and it was stained and scratched with years of neglect. Tramps could often be seen slouching in the doorway, striking matches on the door's worn panels, and schoolboys were fond of carving their names into the wood with their pocket knives.

As the two gentlemen passed, Mr. Enfield raised his walking stick and pointed at the building. "Did you ever notice that ugly door?" he asked.

"Oh, yes," Mr. Utterson replied.

"I have a very odd story to tell, and that door is a part of it," Mr. Enfield told him.

"Really?" Mr. Utterson said with interest. "What is it?"

"I was coming home from a party very late one night," Mr. Enfield began. "It was a black, lonely night, the kind that makes you draw your coat close about you and hurry for the warmth and safety of home. I walked through street after street without seeing a soul—nothing but deserted blocks filled with the shadows from the street lamps. I tell you, after a while I was in such a nervous state that I longed for the sight of a policeman to set my mind at rest! All at once, I saw two figures coming toward each other. One was a little girl about eight years old. She was a shabby child of the streets, running wild on that dark night and not paying the slightest attention to where she was going. The other was a little man who was stomping along very quickly. The two met at the corner."

"What happened?" Mr. Utterson asked.

"A terrible thing," Mr. Enfield replied. "The man trampled over the girl and left her screaming in pain on the ground. Her blood ran onto the street and there were terrible bruises on her body where the man had kicked her. It was horrible to see. The worst of it was that the man didn't stop after he hurt the girl. He just kept walking along as if nothing had happened! It was as if he was a machine. I ran after the fellow, grabbed him by the collar, and brought him back to the corner where the poor girl was still screaming. A crowd had gathered there, including the girl's family and a doctor." Mr. Enfield shook his head. "The girl was not badly hurt, but she was very frightened and upset."

"Naturally," Mr. Utterson said with concern. "What a terrible thing to happen to a child!"

"There was something about the man that made me hate him at first sight," Mr. Enfield admitted. "I wasn't the only one who felt that way. Even the doctor, who was as dry and dull a man as I'd ever met, looked like he wanted to kill the fellow. And it was all we could do to keep the rest of the crowd from ripping him to pieces! I never saw such a group of people eager for revenge. And all the while the man stood there with a black, sneering look on his face, as if he didn't care about what he'd done or how people felt about him."

"Did the man seem sorry?" Mr. Utterson asked.

"Not a bit! We told him that we would make his name stink from one end of London to the other, but he just stood there, calm and unmoved. At last he said, 'If you choose to bring this to the attention of the police, I am helpless to stop you. But like any gentleman, I wish to avoid a scene. Name a price and I will pay it to the girl's family for their trouble.' We talked it over for a bit, and the man finally agreed to give the family one hundred pounds. Then—can you believe it?—the man led us to this very door, whipped out a key, and went inside."

"Did he have the money?" Mr. Utterson asked.

"He had ten pounds in gold and a check for the other ninety pounds. The check was signed by a man whose name I'd rather not mention, but I will say he is one of the most well-known men in London. The whole business seemed rather strange to me, but the fellow just sneered and said, 'Don't worry. The check is good. I will stay with you until the banks open and cash it myself.' And that's just what he did. The horrible man went with the girl's father and myself to the bank. The check was good, and we had no trouble cashing it."

One hundred pounds is equal to several hundred dollars—a huge amount of money in those days.

"How strange," Mr. Utterson muttered.

"It was more than strange," Mr. Enfield replied. "This man was a fellow that no decent person would have anything to do with. Yet the check was signed by one of the most respected men in London, a man who is known for his good deeds and kind nature. I suppose the horrid little man was blackmailing him for some crime he committed when he was young and foolish. Ever since that day, I have called this place Blackmail House." **Blackmail is when you force somebody to pay you so you won't tell anyone about a bad thing the person did.**

"Do you know if the horrid little man lives at this address?" Mr. Utterson asked.

"It seems like the sort of place he would live, doesn't it?" Mr. Enfield replied. "But I happened to notice his address, and it was not in this part of London."

"And you never asked why the man had a key to this building?" Mr. Utterson wondered.

"Of course not! I never ask personal questions if I can help it. You know how it is— you ask one question and that leads to another and another. Pretty soon you know more about a fellow's business than you should. No, my rule is: The stranger something looks, the less I ask."

"That is a very good rule," Mr. Utterson agreed.

"That is such an unusual house," Mr. Enfield went on. "There is no other door except that one I saw the man use that night, yet I've never seen anyone go in or out of the house except him. There are three windows on the other side of the building, but they are always shut. But I've seen smoke coming out of the chimney, so someone must live there. It's a strange street—the houses are so close together that it's hard to say where one ends and another begins."

The two men walked on for a while in silence. Then Mr. Utterson said, "Richard, that rule you have of not asking questions is a good one. But there is one thing I do want to ask. Will you tell me the name of the man who trampled the child?"

"I can't see any harm in telling you that. His name was Hyde."

"What did he look like?"

"It's not easy to describe him. There was something wrong with his appearance— something displeasing and hateful. I have never seen a man I so disliked, yet I don't know why. He must be deformed in some way, inside or out, but I can't put my finger on it. There is nothing out of the ordinary about him, but once you saw him, you would never forget him. No, I can't describe him, although I can see him in my mind as plain as day."

"You're sure he had a key to that door?" Mr. Utterson asked.

"Why, yes," Mr. Enfield said in surprise. "He had a key, and he still has it. I saw him use it not a week ago."

"It is all very peculiar," Mr. Utterson said. "You see, I don't need to ask you the name of the man who signed the check, for I know it already."

Mr. Enfield looked troubled at his friend's words. "Here is another reason to say nothing. I am ashamed at my long tongue and sorry I brought the whole thing up," he said. "Let us promise never to speak of it again."

"I promise that with all my heart," Mr. Utterson said, and the two shook hands to seal the bargain.

Who is the strange man, Mr. Hyde? Why does he have a key to such an odd house? And who is the well-known man who signed the check? These questions are only a small part of this very unusual mystery!

2

Dr. Jekyll's Will

Mr. Utterson was very upset by his conversation with Mr. Enfield. He couldn't even enjoy his supper that evening—and anybody who can't enjoy food must be really worried!

I t was Mr. Utterson's habit to read until bedtime on Sunday evenings, but tonight was different. As soon as he finished his supper, he took a candle and went into his office. There he opened his safe and pulled out an envelope labeled *Dr. Jekyll's Will*.

Mr. Utterson took the envelope over to a table and read through the papers it held. His eyes caught on one section, and he read it over and over again:

In case of the death of Henry Jekyll, M.D., D.C.L., LL.D., F.R.S., **What do all those letters mean? They are abbreviations for all the titles Dr. Jekyll holds. He's a smart and important guy!** *all his possessions are to pass into the hands of his friend, Edward Hyde.*

In case of Dr. Jekyll's disappearance or unexplained absence for any period longer than three months, Edward Hyde shall step into Henry Jekyll's shoes without any trouble or obligation.

Mr. Utterson frowned. He had known Henry Jekyll since they were in school together, more than twenty-five years ago, and there never was a better friend or a kinder, more respected man. Why would a good man like Henry Jekyll leave all his possessions to a hated man like Edward Hyde? Even worse, why would Jekyll make arrangements for this terrible man to take his place? Mr. Utterson hated the terms of this will. There was something about this whole matter that offended his sense of what was right and proper.

"There is certainly something very wrong here," Mr. Utterson said to himself as he replaced the papers in his safe. "At first I thought Jekyll had lost his mind, but now I'm beginning to think he's been disgraced somehow. My friend must be in some kind of trouble."

With that, the lawyer blew out the candle, put on his coat, and headed to the elegant house where his friend, the great Dr. Hastie Lanyon, saw his many patients. "If anyone knows what to make of this, it will be Lanyon," Mr. Utterson told himself.

Dr. Lanyon was a big, hearty man who was always well-dressed and eager for fun. He jumped to his feet when Mr. Utterson entered the room and welcomed him with a firm handshake and a clap on the back that clearly showed how happy he was to see his old friend.

After talking comfortably for a few minutes, Mr. Utterson said, "I suppose you and I must be the two oldest friends that Henry Jekyll has."

"I suppose we are," Dr. Lanyon agreed. "But I see little of him now."

"Really?" Mr. Utterson said in surprise. "I thought you two had a lot in common."

"We did, once," Dr. Lanyon replied. "But it has been more than ten years since Henry Jekyll became a bit too strange for me. He began to talk of such crazy ideas that I could barely understand what he meant. The things he was trying to accomplish made no sense, and they certainly weren't a proper use of his education! In fact, you couldn't get much further from what we doctors were taught to do. I'm still interested in him, for old time's sake, but I cannot agree with his outrageous ideas." The doctor's face flushed with anger as he added, "No respectable man could agree with the unscientific nonsense Jekyll believes to be true!"

They have only disagreed on some point of science, Mr. Utterson thought. *That is not so serious.* Aloud, he asked, "Have you ever met his friend, a man named Hyde?"

"I've never heard of him," Dr. Lanyon said.

Mr. Utterson visited with his old friend for a little while longer, then bid him a fond good-bye and headed home to bed. But the lawyer did not sleep well that night. His dreams were filled with strange images of a man running down a child, and this same man forcing Dr. Jekyll to do some terrible deed. But in all of these dreams, the mysterious Mr. Hyde had no face.

Mr. Utterson woke with a start. He was dizzy with a sick fear for Henry Jekyll. Something terrible was happening—something that seemed to threaten the very life of his oldest and dearest friend!

Mr. Utterson struggled to pull himself together. He was a sensible man, not used to mysteries. If only he could meet Mr. Hyde and see him face to face, then he might be able to understand the strange hold this man had on his friend, Dr. Jekyll.

Will Mr. Utterson be able to find the mysterious Mr. Hyde? Keep reading and see!

3
The Search for Mr. Hyde

Mr. Utterson began to haunt the strange door on that tucked-away side street. Early in the morning, at noontime when the streets were filled with people, in the foggy darkness of night—no matter what time of day, Mr. Utterson could be found neglecting his business to linger near that door, waiting and watching.

If he is Mr. Hyde, the lawyer thought, *then I will be Mr. Seek.*

One fine night, his patience was rewarded. Mr. Utterson waited near the door, shivering a little in the crisp, cold air. The neighborhood was empty, most of its residents tucked into their beds at home. In spite of the low growl of London's traffic in the distance, this particular street was strangely quiet. Mr. Utterson found himself jumping at the slightest noises.

About ten o'clock, Mr. Utterson heard footsteps coming toward him. The steps were oddly distinct in the silent night air. Mr. Utterson had a strange feeling that he was about

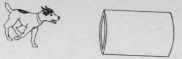

to meet the man he'd been looking for all this time. He ducked into the shadows beside the door and waited.

The steps drew nearer, then swelled out suddenly louder as they turned into the side street. Mr. Utterson looked up and saw a small, plainly dressed man. There was nothing remarkable about him, yet something made Mr. Utterson's blood run cold. It was as if the man wore evil around himself like a black, swirling cloak.

The man walked up to the door and pulled a key out of his pocket. Mr. Utterson stepped forward and touched him on the shoulder. "Mr. Hyde?"

The strange man drew back with a startled hiss. "That is my name," he said after a moment. "What do you want?"

"My name is Mr. Utterson, and I am an old friend of Dr. Jekyll's. He must

Helllooo!
Start flipping the
book pages and check
out the action....
Woo-cha!

31

have mentioned my name to you. May I come in?"

"Dr. Jekyll is away," Mr. Hyde said. "How did you know me?"

"Bear with me for just a moment, please. Will you do me a favor?" Mr. Utterson asked.

"With pleasure," Mr. Hyde replied. "What will it be?"

"Will you let me see your face?"

Mr. Hyde hesitated for a moment. Then he turned around and stared at Mr. Utterson boldly,

as if daring him to look away. But Mr. Utterson did not look away, and the two met each other's gaze for a few moments.

"Now I shall know you should we meet again," Mr. Utterson said at last. "That may be useful."

"Yes," Mr. Hyde agreed. "It is good that we have met. Let me give you my address." He told Utterson the name and number of a house in Soho. **Soho is a neighborhood in London. In those days, it was a shabby neighborhood—dirty and run-down, with dingy homes and people crowding its narrow streets. It was definitely not the sort of place rich men like Mr. Utterson hung around!**

Why is he giving me his address? Mr. Utterson thought. *Can he be letting me know how to contact him because of the terms of Dr. Jekyll's will?* The thought that Mr. Hyde wanted to be sure to get Dr. Jekyll's money disgusted the lawyer, but he did not feel it was his place to say anything.

"Now, how did you know me?" Mr. Hyde asked.

"By description," Mr. Utterson replied. "We have common friends."

"Common friends?" Mr. Hyde repeated in surprise. "Who?"

"Dr. Jekyll, for instance."

"He never told you about me," Mr. Hyde said angrily. "I did not think a man such as you would lie!"

"Here now, that is not a nice thing to say," Mr. Utterson said, offended.

Mr. Hyde snarled a savage laugh. Then he quickly unlocked the door and disappeared inside the mysterious house.

For some moments after Mr. Hyde had left, Mr. Utterson stood there. He was greatly troubled. Mr. Hyde had been rude to him, but that alone was not enough to explain the disgust and hatred Mr. Utterson felt. "The man seems hardly human," he said to himself, "although there is nothing in his body to suggest that anything is wrong. There is something inside of him, some darkness in his soul that makes him so hard to look at." He shook his head. "Poor Henry Jekyll," he whispered. "If ever I saw the face of evil, it is on his friend."

Mr. Utterson walked around the corner. There was a square filled with old houses there. **Many parts of London have streets arranged into a square, with**

34

a garden or a small park in the center. Most of the houses had suffered from the passage of time, and they had a decayed, sad look about them. But one house still wore an air of great wealth and comfort, although right now it was plunged in darkness. Mr. Utterson went up the steps of this fine home and knocked on the door. A well-dressed butler answered.

"Good evening, Poole," Mr. Utterson said. "Is Dr. Jekyll at home?"

"Let me see," the butler said. "Come in, please." He led Mr. Utterson into a large, comfortable room filled with expensive furniture. A fire blazed in the hearth.

Mr. Utterson had often called this room "the pleasantest room in London." But that night there was a shudder in his blood, and the face of Mr. Hyde sat heavily in his mind. Mr. Utterson was a cheerful man, but tonight, for the first time, he felt tired and sick of life. The fire was not welcoming and warm tonight—Mr. Utterson's gloom had filled it with flickering shadows and danger.

Poole returned after a few minutes and announced that Dr. Jekyll had gone out.

"That door in the side street behind the

house," Mr. Utterson began. "Doesn't it lead to Dr. Jekyll's laboratory?"

"Yes, sir."

"I saw Mr. Hyde going in there just now," Mr. Utterson said. "Is it all right for him to be there when Dr. Jekyll is not at home?"

"Oh, yes, that's quite all right, Mr. Utterson," Poole replied. "Mr. Hyde has a key."

"Dr. Jekyll seems to trust Mr. Hyde a great deal."

"Yes, he does," the butler said. "All the servants have orders to obey him. But we see very little of him in this part of the house. He always comes and goes through the laboratory."

"All right, then. Good night, Poole," Mr. Utterson said.

The lawyer headed home with a heavy heart. "Poor Henry Jekyll," he said. "He must be in great danger! I remember that he was a little wild when he was young. We both were." Mr. Utterson thought for a few minutes of the many bad things he had done in the past, although he knew he had led a fairly blameless life compared to most people. Still, it only took one wrong move to ruin a man's reputation for the rest of his life.

"Perhaps Henry went too far at one time," Mr. Utterson continued. "Perhaps he is haunted by the ghost of some crime he committed—a crime that Mr. Hyde is threatening to tell the world about."

Suddenly Mr. Utterson felt a spark of hope. "This Mr. Hyde must have secrets of his own," he said. "They must be terrible secrets! Why, I am sure that Henry Jekyll's worst crime would seem like sunshine compared to the dark deeds that little man has done. If I can only find them out, perhaps I can save Henry after all."

Mr. Utterson shook his head. "It turns me cold to think of that creature sneaking into Henry's home and standing over him while he sleeps. If Hyde knows that the terms of Jekyll's will say he is to inherit everything, I am sure he would stop at nothing—even murder—to get Henry's fortune!"

As Mr. Utterson entered his own house, he made a promise. "I must do something to save poor Henry Jekyll—if he will only let me!"

Mr. Utterson is sure that his old friend is in grave danger. But can he do anything to help him? Things are more complicated than anyone realizes!

4
Dinner with Dr. Jekyll

We've heard a lot about Dr. Henry Jekyll. In this chapter we finally get to meet the mysterious doctor and hear what he has to say about Mr. Hyde.

Two weeks after Mr. Utterson met Mr. Hyde, Dr. Jekyll gave a dinner party for several of his old friends—all intelligent, respectable men. Of course, Mr. Utterson was included. Everyone had a fine evening.

Mr. Utterson made a point of staying after all the other guests had gone. This was not unusual, for hosts were always happy to talk with him after all the other guests had left. After all the light-hearted silliness that went on at parties, people were glad to relax with Mr. Utterson and share his quiet company. Dr. Jekyll was no exception, and Mr. Utterson welcomed the chance to talk with his friend in private.

The lawyer and the doctor settled in front of

the fire. Dr. Jekyll was a large, strongly built man of about fifty. There was a mischievous light in his eyes, as if he enjoyed a good joke or a prank, but he was clearly a kind-hearted and generous man. Anyone could tell just by looking at him that he was very fond of Mr. Utterson and always glad of his company.

"I have been wanting to speak with you for some time, Henry," Mr. Utterson said at last. "You know that will of yours?"

Dr. Jekyll tried to hide his unhappiness regarding this subject matter. "I have never seen anyone as upset as you are over that will!" he exclaimed. "You make as much fuss over it as Dr. Lanyon does when he complains about my scientific ideas. He is the most stubborn, narrow-minded man I have ever met!"

"Dr. Lanyon has nothing to do with this. You know I never approved of the terms of that will," Mr. Utterson went on.

"Yes, you have told me that from the beginning," Dr. Jekyll said sharply.

"Well, now I am telling you again," Mr. Utterson said. "You see, I have been learning about your friend, Mr. Hyde."

Dr. Jekyll's handsome face grew very pale, and a hard look came into his eyes. "I do not care to hear any more," he said. "I thought we had agreed not to discuss this matter."

"What I have heard about Mr. Hyde is horrible," Mr. Utterson continued.

"It doesn't matter," Dr. Jekyll said firmly. "You don't understand my position. I am in a very unusual situation—one that cannot be fixed by talking about it."

"Henry, you know you can trust me," Mr. Utterson said. "Confess whatever it is that you've done, and your secret will be safe with me. Whatever the trouble is, I am sure I can get you out of it."

"That is very kind of you, my friend," Dr. Jekyll replied. "I trust you more than any man alive—even more than I trust myself—but things really aren't as bad as you think. If it will make you rest easier, I will tell you that the moment I choose, I can be rid of Mr. Hyde forever. I give you my word. Now, this is a private matter, so please let us not discuss it again."

Utterson stared into the fire for a few moments, thinking over Dr. Jekyll's words. "If you

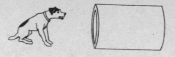

insist," he said at last. "I just hope you are right about Mr. Hyde." Thinking there was no more to say, the lawyer got to his feet.

"Since we are talking about the subject, let me just say one more thing about this matter—the last thing, I hope," Dr. Jekyll said. "I have taken a great interest in Mr. Hyde, and I am concerned for his future. You must promise me that if anything should happen to me, you will make sure Mr. Hyde gets his rights according to the will."

"I can't pretend that I like the man," Mr. Utterson said.

"I'm not asking you to like him," Dr. Jekyll responded. "I only ask for justice. I only ask you to help him for my sake, when I am no longer here."

Utterson sighed. "All right," he said reluctantly. "I promise."

I have a bad feeling about this whole matter—and so does Mr. Utterson! The lawyer has good reason to dislike Mr. Hyde. That wicked man is capable of anything, as we are about to see.

5
Murder!

A whole year goes by without anything unusual happening. Then, late one night, all of London is shocked by a terrible crime.

It was after eleven o'clock on a moonlit October night. A young maidservant who lived in a house near the river was looking out of her window. The full moon lit the street below, making everything look sharp and clear. It was such a beautiful evening that the maid felt at peace with the world.

As she sat lost in her dreamy thoughts, the maid saw an elderly gentleman walking along the street. He was quite handsome and distinguished, with a head full of shining white hair.

As the maid watched, a short, squat man hurried along the street. He met the first man right under the maid's window, and the older man bowed to him politely. The maid was surprised to see that the smaller man was a fellow who had visited her master once. His

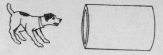

name was Mr. Hyde, and she had disliked him immediately, although she could not explain why she felt that way.

The first gentleman said something to Mr. Hyde in a courteous voice. The maid was charmed by his manners—the gentleman was so polite and kind! Mr. Hyde did not answer the old man. He just fingered his heavy walking stick as if he were impatient and did not want to listen to him.

Suddenly Mr. Hyde burst into a great flame of anger. He stamped his feet and began waving the walking stick like a madman. The old gentleman stepped back, looking surprised and hurt.

Then the maid saw a horrible thing. Mr. Hyde raised his walking stick and clubbed the old man to the ground with a savage blow. Then he jumped on the body and began to trample it while he struck even more blows with his heavy stick. The old man's bones crunched and shattered under this terrible attack, and his body twisted and jerked with agony. The maid was so horrified at the sight and sounds that she fainted.

When she woke hours later, the street was quiet. The murderer was gone, but the mangled body of his victim still lay in the middle of the

street. Shaking and sick, the maid called for the police.

The murder weapon—the heavy walking stick—had snapped in two, and a piece lay in the gutter. The police found some money and a fine gold watch on the victim, along with an envelope addressed to Mr. Gabriel John Utterson. It seemed that the gentleman had been on his way to mail

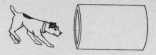

the letter to Mr. Utterson when he was killed.

One of the police inspectors—a man named Newcomen—hurried to the lawyer's house early the next morning and got him out of bed. When Utterson heard the story, he looked very serious. "I shall say nothing until I have seen the body," he said firmly. Then he dressed, ate a quick breakfast, and went off to the police station, where the body had been taken.

As soon as Utterson saw the body, he nodded. "Yes," he said. "I know him. I'm sorry to say that this is Sir Danvers Carew."

"What?" exclaimed Inspector Newcomen. Sir Danvers Carew was a Member of Parliament, and one of the best-known and respected men in all of London. "This is going to make a great deal of noise," Inspector Newcomen continued. "Perhaps you can help us track down the

> Parliament is the group of people that makes the laws in England. A Member of Parliament, or M.P., is a very important person.

killer. The maid said his name is Mr. Hyde, and he was carrying this walking stick."

Mr. Utterson shuddered when he heard Mr. Hyde's name. When the walking stick was laid before him, he was even more shocked. Broken and battered as it was, he recognized the stick as one he had himself given to Henry Jekyll many years ago. "Is this Mr. Hyde a small man?" he asked.

"Particularly small and particularly wicked-looking—that's how the maid described him," the inspector said.

Mr. Utterson sighed heavily. "I think I can take you to his home," he said.

The two men stepped into Mr. Utterson's carriage and headed toward the Soho address that Mr. Hyde had given Mr. Utterson the night they met more than a year ago. The lawyer thought the neighborhood looked like something out of a nightmare. A heavy, chocolate-colored fog hung over the city, swirling into monstrous forms in the wind. The muddy street where Mr. Hyde lived was crowded with dirty stores and shabby houses. Ragged, half-starved children huddled in the doorways, and the dim light of the street lamps

cast horrifying shadows into the thick, damp air. Utterson could hardly believe that this was the home of Henry Jekyll's friend and heir to his large fortune.

A silver-haired old woman opened the door. Her face was harsh and cruel, but good manners smoothed her expression into one of forced pleasantness. "Yes, this is Mr. Hyde's house, but he is not at home," she snapped in answer to Mr. Utterson's question. "He came in late last night and left very soon after."

"Did that seem strange to you?" Mr. Utterson asked.

"Oh, no. He often comes and goes at odd hours. He's absent a lot of the time too. Before last night, I hadn't seen him in almost two months."

"Very well, then. We wish to inspect his rooms," Mr. Utterson said.

"I cannot allow you—"

"This is Inspector Newcomen of Scotland Yard," Mr. Utterson interrupted. **Scotland Yard was the name of the street where the London police department was located. In time, the term "Scotland Yard" became a kind of nickname for the London police.**

"Is Mr. Hyde in trouble?" the housekeeper

said, looking delighted at the thought. "What has he done?"

Mr. Utterson and Inspector Newcomen looked at each other. "He certainly isn't a popular man," the inspector commented. To the woman, he said, "Please let us have a look around."

To Mr. Utterson's surprise, the house was empty except for a few rooms which Mr. Hyde had furnished with elegance and good taste. The furniture was well-made out of the most expensive woods, and there was a beautiful painting on the wall. Mr. Utterson was sure the painting was a gift from Henry Jekyll, whose eye for valuable artwork was well-known.

It was plain to see that Mr. Hyde had taken what he could and left in a great hurry. Clothes were scattered all over the floor, their pockets turned inside out. The desk drawers were open, and a pile of ashes in the hearth showed that some papers recently had been burned there.

Inspector Newcomen found the other half of the walking stick behind the door. "Very good," the policeman said with great satisfaction. "This confirms our suspicions that Mr. Hyde committed the crime." Mr. Utterson nodded. He was filled

with dread at this evidence that proved Mr. Hyde was indeed a vicious murderer.

Inspector Newcomen sifted through the ashes of the fire and found part of Mr. Hyde's checkbook. There were several thousand pounds in the account. **That would be more than fifty thousand dollars today. What a fortune!**

"We will catch Mr. Hyde soon—you can depend on that," the inspector said with pleasure. "He must have panicked and lost his head to be stupid enough to leave the walking stick and his checkbook behind. This sort of man won't be able to get by without money. All we have to do is wait for him at the bank. In the meantime, we'll send handbills around to try and find where he's hiding." **A handbill is a poster with the picture of a criminal, along with a description of him. It's like a "wanted" poster.**

But the handbills could not be made. Although many people had seen Mr. Hyde, no one could really describe him, and the few descriptions the police did get were very different

49

from each other. The only things everyone could agree on were that Mr. Hyde was a small man, and that there was something haunting and disturbing about him. There were no photographs of him anywhere, and no one had seen him since the night of the murder. It was as if Sir Carew's killer had disappeared into thin air.

6
Clues in a Letter

Does Dr. Jekyll realize that his friend, Mr. Hyde, has committed a murder? That's exactly what Mr. Utterson wants to know!

Late that same day, Mr. Utterson went to Dr. Jekyll's door. The butler, Poole, let him in. "Come with me, sir," he said, and led Mr. Utterson through the kitchen to the back of the house to Dr. Jekyll's laboratory— the room hidden behind the mysterious door.

Mr. Utterson had never been in this part of his friend's house before. The men's footsteps echoed strangely in the large, high-ceilinged room. There were no windows to let in the cheer of daylight. Shadows loomed in the corners and leaped out to snatch at Mr. Utterson as he moved through the vast emptiness. He looked around at the tables covered with bottles of chemicals and packets of powder, at the boxes stacked everywhere on the floor. This laboratory was shockingly different from the elegant rooms in the rest of the house! It was almost as if a different creature than the smart and stylish doctor lived here.

Poole led Mr. Utterson into an office behind the laboratory. A large mirror stood in one corner, seeming out of place among the work tables. Three dusty windows barred with iron looked out over the courtyard.

Mr. Utterson stopped in surprise. There, sitting close to the fire as if he could not get warm enough, was Dr. Henry Jekyll. He looked deathly sick. Mr. Utterson rushed to his side, horrified at the sight of his friend. Dr. Jekyll did not stand to greet his visitor—he only held out a cold hand. "Hello, Gabriel," he said in a weak voice.

"Have you heard the news?" Mr. Utterson said as soon as Poole had left the room.

The doctor shuddered. "I heard the newsboys crying it in the square," he said. **In the old days, boys sold newspapers on the street corners. They would call out the headlines to attract customers.**

"Just tell me one thing. Carew was my client, but so are you, and I want to know where things

stand. You have not been foolish enough to hide the murderer, have you?" Mr. Utterson demanded.

"I swear to you, I will never set eyes on Mr. Hyde again!" Dr. Jekyll cried. "I am done with him. Indeed, he does not want my help. He is quite safe. Mark my words, he will never be heard of again."

The lawyer listened to his friend's words with dismay, for he did not like Dr. Jekyll's excited manner. "You seem very sure of this," Mr. Utterson commented.

"For your sake, I hope you are right. If Mr. Hyde is brought to trial, your name could well appear."

Mr. Utterson is pointing out the danger to Dr. Jekyll's reputation here. If he were mentioned as part of a murder trial, his good name would be ruined!

"I am sure. I know Mr. Hyde quite well, you see," the doctor said. "Look, I have received a letter from him. I will give it to you, and you may do what you think best with it. I know you will make the right decision, for I have great trust in you."

"I suppose you fear that this note might lead the police to Mr. Hyde," Mr. Utterson said.

"No," replied the doctor. "I don't care what happens to Mr. Hyde. I am done with the man! Actually, I was thinking of the damage this nasty business might do to my own character."

Mr. Utterson was surprised at his friend's selfishness. How could he think only of his own reputation when a man lay savagely murdered? But a part of him was relieved as well, for Dr. Jekyll's concern for his reputation made him seem less crazed and strange. "All right," the lawyer said. "Let me see the letter."

Dr. Jekyll handed Mr. Utterson a piece of paper. It read:

Dear Dr. Jekyll,

You have always been very helpful to me, and I can never repay you for your generosity. You need not worry about my safety now, for I have a sure means of escape.

Edward Hyde

Mr. Utterson was filled with relief as he read these words. This letter made it sound as if Dr. Jekyll was just helping out a man in need. There

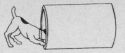

was no sign of a threat or blackmail. *Perhaps I should not have suspected the worst after all*, Mr. Utterson thought, feeling guilty. He studied the murderer's signature, which was written in an odd, upright hand. "Do you have the envelope?" he asked.

"No, I burned it before I thought better of it. But it bore no postmark. The note must have been brought by a messenger."

"I want to ask you one question," Mr. Utterson said. "Did Mr. Hyde force you to write your will so that he would inherit everything if you ever disappeared?"

The question seemed to terrify Dr. Jekyll. He leaned back in his chair and looked like he might faint. Then he swallowed hard and nodded.

"I knew it," Mr. Utterson said. "He meant to murder you. You have had a narrow escape."

"I have had a lesson," Dr. Jekyll replied. "Oh, what a lesson I have had!" He covered his face with his hands.

On his way out, Mr. Utterson stopped to talk to Poole. "Dr. Jekyll received a letter today," he said. "Who was the messenger?"

"Nothing came by messenger today, sir," said

Poole, looking surprised. "There were no letters in the mail today either—only advertisements."

Mr. Utterson was troubled by this news. It seemed Mr. Hyde's note had come by the laboratory door. It might even have been written right in Dr. Jekyll's office! Had Mr. Hyde threatened Dr. Jekyll into writing the note? Mr. Utterson shuddered at the horrifying picture that sprang into his mind—Mr. Hyde looming over the helpless doctor and threatening murder if he did not do as Mr. Hyde demanded!

"Special edition!" the newsboys were shouting. "Shocking murder of an M.P.!" Mr. Utterson listened to their cries with dread. They were speaking of the death of his friend and client. He wondered if the good name of another friend—Henry Jekyll—would soon be sucked down into the darkness of this crime.

"What should I do?" Mr. Utterson asked himself. "If I help catch Sir Carew's murder, I may harm Henry Jekyll, my closest friend! If only someone could give me advice on how to solve this ticklish problem." It was hard for the lawyer to ask for another person's help, for he had always depended on himself. But this case

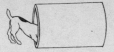

was too important to let his pride get in the way.

Mr. Utterson went home and sat down before the fire. His head clerk, Mr. Guest, came in and sat beside him, for the two were old friends. Mr. Utterson was glad to be inside, in the company of a friend beside a comforting fire. Outside, the fog still hung over the city, lit here and there by the hazy glow of the street lamps. The gloomy air rang with the roar of London traffic, as if some great, harsh wind were racing through the streets.

Mr. Utterson had no secrets from Mr. Guest, and his worry about Dr. Jekyll's involvement in Sir Carew's murder weighed upon him heavily. He found himself telling Mr. Guest all about his visit with Dr. Jekyll. Mr. Utterson was sure that his clerk would provide him with some comment or insight that would help Mr. Utterson decide what to do next.

"This is a sad business about Sir Carew," Mr. Utterson said.

"Yes, it is indeed," Mr. Guest replied. "It has stirred up a great deal of public feeling. The murderer, of course, was crazy."

"I should like to hear your views on that

matter," Mr. Utterson said. "I have a letter written in the murderer's hand, and I know you are a great student of handwriting. This note must be a secret between you and me, for I hardly know what to do about it. This is such an ugly business. But here it is—a murderer's autograph. What do you make of it?"

Mr. Guest's eyes brightened as Mr. Utterson handed him the note. The clerk studied it for a long moment. "No, I don't think the writer is crazy," he said at last. "But I will say this is written in a very odd hand."

"From what I know, the writer is a very odd man," Mr. Utterson commented.

Just then, a servant entered with a note for Mr. Utterson. Mr. Guest glanced at the handwriting on the envelope. "Is that from Dr. Jekyll?" he asked. When Mr. Utterson nodded, the clerk added, "I thought I recognized the writing. Is it anything private?"

"No, just an invitation to dinner," Mr. Utterson replied. "Why? Do you want to see it?"

"Yes, I do." Mr. Guest laid the sheet of paper beside the note from Mr. Hyde and carefully compared the two. "Very interesting," he remarked.

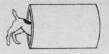

"Why do you say that?" Mr. Utterson asked.

"The handwriting is very much the same. Only the slant of the letters is different. Otherwise, the two are practically identical!"

"How strange," Mr. Utterson said. From what Mr. Guest had said, Mr. Utterson had the feeling Dr. Jekyll might have forged the note from Mr. Hyde. **A forgery is when someone writes and signs a document in another person's handwriting.** "Mr. Guest, please don't speak of this note to anyone."

"Of course not," the clerk agreed.

After his friend had left, Mr. Utterson put the note in his safe. His hands were trembling so hard that they could barely turn the dial to lock the horrible paper out of sight. "Why would Henry Jekyll forge a letter from a murderer?" he asked himself. The very thought made his blood run cold in his veins.

What's going on here? Did Dr. Jekyll write that note from Mr. Hyde? And how can he be so sure that Mr. Hyde is gone forever? I think the doctor knows a lot more than he's telling!

7
Strange Behavior

Months passed. In spite of the huge reward offered for the capture of Edward Hyde, the murderer could not be found. Many people came forward with stories of the man's past and the many hateful, cruel things he had done, but there was not so much as a hint as to where he might be. Even the police, who had tracked down many a criminal, had never seen anything like this complete disappearance. From the time he left his house in Soho on the morning of the murder, there was no trace of Mr. Hyde anywhere. It was as if he no longer existed.

Now that the evil influence of Mr. Hyde was gone, Dr. Jekyll was like a new man. He began to appear in public once more. He took up with his old friends, went to parties, and seemed to be enjoying life again.

On January 8, Dr. Jekyll invited Mr. Utterson and several others to his house for dinner. Dr. Jekyll's old friend, Dr. Lanyon, was also there, and it seemed as if any disagreements between the two

had been forgotten. Everyone had a merry evening. *It was just like old times*, Mr. Utterson thought happily as he went home that night.

But when Mr. Utterson went to visit Dr. Jekyll on January 12, he was turned away at the door. The same thing happened over the next few days. "Dr. Jekyll will see no one," Poole told him.

Mr. Utterson was very worried. "For the past few months, Dr. Jekyll has been out and about, enjoying the presence of his friends," he said to himself. "Now he has shut himself up alone again. I do not like this at all."

Along with his worry about Dr. Jekyll's sudden change of mood, Mr. Utterson missed his friend's company. He had enjoyed Dr. Jekyll's company almost every day for the past two months. Now, as the days passed without any word from the doctor, Mr. Utterson felt lonelier than ever.

The lawyer decided to visit his old friend, Dr. Lanyon. Perhaps he had some idea of what had happened to Dr. Jekyll.

When Mr. Utterson walked into Dr. Lanyon's house, he received a terrible shock. Dr. Lanyon, once so hearty and healthy, now looked desperately sick. At the moment he set eyes on the doctor, Mr. Utterson was sure his friend was going to die soon. Dr. Lanyon was pale and terribly thin, as if the flesh had melted away from his bones. Much of his hair had fallen out as well. Even worse, there was a terrified look in his eye, as if he had seen something too horrible to bear.

"My dear friend, you look quite ill!" Mr. Utterson said.

"I have had a shock, and I shall never recover," Dr. Lanyon told him. "I know I only have a few weeks left. Life has been pleasant, and I liked it very much. But if a person knows too much, life is not so wonderful. Yes, I am a doomed man."

"Dr. Jekyll is ill too," Mr. Utterson said. "Have you seen him?"

At the mention of Dr. Jekyll's name, Dr. Lanyon held up a hand that shook violently. "I wish to see or hear no more of Dr. Jekyll," he said in an unsteady voice. "I am done with that person, and I beg you not to mention his name to me again. As far as I am concerned, Dr. Jekyll is dead!"

"Now, now." Mr. Utterson tried to calm his friend, although he disapproved of Dr. Lanyon's lack of sympathy for Dr. Jekyll's illness. "Just last week, the three of us dined together and had a very good time. Can't I do anything to mend this friendship?" he asked quietly. "We three have been friends for too long to have it end like this."

"Nothing can be done," Dr. Lanyon insisted. "Ask Dr. Jekyll himself."

"He will not see me," the lawyer admitted.

"I am not surprised. Someday, after I am dead, you may come to learn the right and wrong of what has happened, but I cannot tell you now," Dr. Lanyon said. "In the meantime, if you can sit and talk with me of other things, I would like that very much. But if you cannot help talking about that cursed Dr. Jekyll, I must ask you to leave, for I cannot bear to think about him!"

"Very well," Mr. Utterson agreed reluctantly. He stayed a little while longer at Dr. Lanyon's side, talking of this and that. But the lawyer barely knew what he was saying. It was hard to concentrate when his mind was filled with worry over Dr. Lanyon's terrible—and mysterious—illness. And he still was no closer to understanding what was wrong with Dr. Jekyll, or what had caused the terrible fight between him and Dr. Lanyon.

By the time Mr. Utterson walked home that night, he was more troubled than ever. Events seemed to be going from bad to worse, and he had no idea how to make things right again.

What has happened to make Dr. Lanyon so sick? And why is he so angry at Dr. Jekyll? This mystery is getting more and more perplexing!

8
Dr. Jekyll's Explanation

As soon as he got home from Dr. Lanyon's that night, Mr. Utterson sat down and wrote a letter to Dr. Jekyll. He demanded an explanation for why the doctor had refused to see him, and he also asked what had happened between Dr. Jekyll and Dr. Lanyon to cause their terrible fight. The very next day, the lawyer received Dr. Jekyll's reply.

Mr. Utterson quickly unfolded the pages of Dr. Jekyll's letter. What he read there did not ease his mind one bit. Dr. Jekyll wrote:

> To be secluded means to be alone. Dr. Jekyll is going to live apart from other people.

The quarrel with Lanyon cannot be cured. I do not blame our old friend, but I share his view that we must never meet again. From now on I will live a life of seclusion. Do not be surprised or unhappy if my door is often closed to you. It is nothing you have done to make me act this way. Believe me when I say that I still value you as a trusted friend, but I must go my own dark way. I have brought on myself a punishment and a danger that I cannot name. The only way you can help me is to respect my silence and leave me to myself.

There was more to the letter, but Mr. Utterson could not understand it. Dr. Jekyll's words were strange and mysterious, and Mr. Utterson could get no sense out of them.

But one thing was clear—his friend was in a very sad frame of mind. Mr. Utterson was amazed at the change in him. For the past few months, the dark influence of Mr. Hyde had disappeared, and Dr. Jekyll had been as cheerful and happy as Mr. Utterson had ever seen him. Now it seemed as if everything good in the doctor's life—peace of mind, friendship, joy—had been swept away. Mr. Utterson could only think of one thing that could cause so great a change in such a short time. Dr. Jekyll must be losing his mind.

The following week, Dr. Lanyon became so ill that he took to his bed. Less than two weeks later, he was dead.

Dr. Lanyon's funeral was a sad affair. As Mr. Utterson stood beside the grave in the rain, he wondered what had happened to cause Dr. Lanyon's sudden death. He could not help but think that Dr. Lanyon's last conversation with Dr. Jekyll had something to do with Lanyon's illness. But what on earth could Dr. Jekyll have told him that was terrible enough to kill him?

The night after Dr. Lanyon's funeral, Mr. Utterson went into his office and locked the door behind him. He lit a candle and took from his pocket an envelope addressed to him in Dr. Lanyon's handwriting. Setting it down on the desk, he stared at it for a long moment.

Private, read the words on the front of the envelope. *For the hands of G. J. Utterson alone. In case of his death, to be destroyed unread. Signed, Dr. Hastie Lanyon.*

Mr. Utterson held the envelope in his hands for a long moment, but he could not make his fingers tear the packet open. Something held him back—some dark dread that told him bad news lay within. "Go ahead, man, do your duty," he muttered to himself at last, and broke the seal.

Inside was another sealed envelope. On this, Dr. Lanyon had written: *Not to be opened until the death or disappearance of Dr. Henry Jekyll.*

Mr. Utterson could not believe his eyes. *Death or disappearance.* Those were the very same words Dr. Jekyll had written in his will! But hadn't the terms of the will been forced on Dr. Jekyll by Mr. Hyde, who had long since disappeared? Why would Dr. Lanyon need to write about a possible disappearance here?

More than anything, Utterson wanted to open that envelope and read its contents. *Dr. Lanyon is dead,* a voice whispered in his mind. *He will not know if you disobey his wishes and open this envelope. And whatever is inside there might give you some clues to help Dr. Jekyll!*

No, you must not open that envelope, another voice whispered back. *Dr. Lanyon himself wrote that this was not to be opened until Dr. Jekyll is gone. It is your duty as his lawyer—and his friend— to follow his wishes.*

In the end, Mr. Utterson's sense of duty won the battle. He placed the sealed envelope in his safe and locked the door.

I can't stand it! What is in that envelope? I just know it's the answer to the mystery. Mr. Utterson may have locked Dr. Lanyon's letter inside his safe, but he can't stop thinking about what it might contain. Now he is more sure than ever that Dr. Jekyll is mixed up in something terrible.

9
Meeting at the Window

O ver the next few weeks, Mr. Utterson tried to visit Dr. Jekyll many times. Each time, he was turned away by the doctor's butler, Poole.

"I'm sorry, sir," Poole told him one day. "I cannot give you any good news about the doctor. He spends almost all his time in the office in his laboratory now. Sometimes he even sleeps there. I don't know what he does in there all day—he hardly ever speaks to anyone. I think he has something terrible on his mind."

In time, Mr. Utterson became discouraged, and he visited less and less. To be honest, he was a bit relieved at not being able to see his friend, for he was worried about what he might find. It was much more pleasant to stand on the doorstep speaking with Poole, surrounded by the fresh air and the sounds of the city, rather than be trapped within the lonely walls with a recluse. **A recluse is someone who can't stand to be around other people. Sadly, that's just what Dr. Jekyll has become.**

One Sunday, Mr. Utterson was taking his usual walk with his friend, Mr. Enfield. The two happened to pass the side street with the ugly door—the door both men had seen Mr. Hyde use.

"Well, that story is at an end, at least," Mr. Enfield said. "I think we shall never see Mr. Hyde again."

"I hope not," Mr. Utterson said. "Did I ever tell you that I saw him once? I felt the same sickening disgust you did."

"It was impossible not to hate the man on sight," Mr. Enfield agreed. "By the way, I certainly was surprised when I found out that this was the back door to Dr. Jekyll's house. How strange that those two should know each other!"

"Yes," Mr. Utterson agreed. "Let us step into the courtyard and have a look in Jekyll's windows. To tell you the truth, I am worried about the poor man. I think it would do him good to see us, even if we just wave to him through the window."

The two men went around into the little courtyard where the three windows looked into Dr. Jekyll's office. The middle window was halfway open. Sitting inside was Dr. Jekyll, looking as

heartbroken and lonely as a prisoner shut away from the light of day.

"How good to see you!" Mr. Utterson exclaimed at the sight of his friend. "I hope you are feeling better."

"No, I am very sick," Dr. Jekyll responded in a quiet voice. "I will not last long, thank goodness."

"You stay indoors too much," Mr. Utterson said. "You need some fresh air. Come now, get your coat and hat and take a walk with us!"

"You are kind to ask me," Dr. Jekyll said, "and I would like very much to come along. But no, it's impossible. I dare not do it." He sighed heavily. "I *am* glad to see you. I would ask you in, but the place is really not fixed up for company."

"Well then, we can stay right here and speak with you through the window," Mr. Utterson said.

"That is just what I was about to say," the doctor said with a smile. But the words were hardly out of his mouth when the smile was ripped from his face. In its place was such a look of terror and despair that it froze the blood of both Mr. Utterson and Mr. Enfield. Dr. Jekyll slammed the window shut, but it was too late. His visitors had seen the strange, twisted horror on the doctor's face all too clearly.

The gentlemen hurried out of the courtyard without a word. It wasn't until they had reached the busy main street and were surrounded by the cheerful bustle of the crowds again that Mr.

Utterson glanced at his friend's face. Mr. Enfield was pale and his eyes were filled with fear, as if he had just seen something too monstrous to speak of. Mr. Utterson knew his own face bore a look of answering fright. A look of sheer terror passed between them.

"God help the poor man," Mr. Utterson murmured. Mr. Enfield nodded. Then the two walked on in silence—a silence filled with dread.

Mr. Utterson and Mr. Enfield have received a terrible shock! Mr. Utterson doesn't even know how to help Dr. Jekyll now. Things have gone much too far! Be warned—things are about to get even stranger—and very dangerous!

10
Foul Play?

Mr. Utterson was sitting by his fireside one evening when he was surprised to receive a visit from Poole.

"Bless me, Poole, what brings you here?" the lawyer asked. Dr. Jekyll's butler had never come to his house before. Then the lawyer took another look at Poole's face and saw that the man was very upset. "What is the matter?" Mr. Utterson asked. "Is the doctor ill?"

"Mr. Utterson," said the butler, "there is something wrong."

"Have a seat," Mr. Utterson urged. "Let me pour you a drink. Now take your time and tell me what is going on."

"You know the doctor's ways, and how he has shut himself away from the world," Poole began. "Well, he's shut up in the office in his laboratory again, and I don't like it." The butler took a deep breath. "I am afraid."

"Now, my good man, tell me more. Exactly what are you afraid of?" Mr. Utterson asked.

"I've been afraid for about a week," Poole said. "I can bear it no longer."

The man certainly *seemed* afraid. He was jumpy and nervous, and he could not look Mr. Utterson in the face. Even now he sat with his drink untasted beside him, his eyes staring into a corner of the floor. "I can bear it no longer," he repeated.

"Come now, Poole, I can see you have good reason to be afraid," the lawyer said patiently. "Something terrible must have happened. Try to tell me what it is."

"I think there has been foul play."

"Foul play!" Mr. Utterson repeated. He was beginning to feel afraid himself. "What do you mean?"

"I dare not say," Poole replied. "But will you come with me and see for yourself?"

Mr. Utterson's answer was to snatch up his hat and coat. Poole's face lit up with relief and thankfulness when he realized Mr. Utterson was going to help him. The two men hurried out into the street.

It was a wild, cold March night. A strong wind whistled down the streets, making talking difficult and bringing color to the men's cheeks. The moon lay on its back as if the wind had blown it over.

Mr. Utterson had never seen the streets so empty. He wished some people were out and about. In fact, never in his life had he felt the need to see and touch others and find comfort in their presence. His mind was filled with a sense of coming doom.

The streets of the square where Dr. Jekyll lived were filled with wind and dust. The thin trees in the garden were lashing themselves along the railing. Poole, who had been walking a few steps ahead of the lawyer, stopped suddenly in the middle of the sidewalk. In spite of the bitter cold, he took off his hat and wiped the sweat from his forehead with a handkerchief. His face was white as a ghost's, and when he spoke, his voice was harsh and broken.

"Well, sir," the butler said, "here we are. God grant that there is nothing wrong."

"Amen," Mr. Utterson agreed.

Poole knocked nervously on the door of his master's house, and the door was opened a tiny crack. "Is that you, Poole?" one of the servants whispered.

"It's all right," Poole answered. "Open the door."

They entered the hall. The fire was burning brightly, and all of the servants were huddled before it like a flock of sheep. At the sight of Mr. Utterson, one of the maids burst into tears. The cook cried out, "Thank God Mr. Utterson is here!" and ran forward as if she were about to fling her arms around him.

"What is going on here?" Mr. Utterson asked sharply. "Why are you neglecting your work? Your master would be far from pleased at your behavior."

"They are all afraid, sir," Poole explained. Indeed, the servants were all staring at the inner door with dreadful expectation, as if they were sure some horrible monster would leap out and destroy them all.

Poole picked up a candle and motioned Mr. Utterson to follow him to the back of the house. The two men walked through the kitchen and down the hall toward Dr. Jekyll's laboratory. "Now, sir," Mr. Poole said. "I want you to listen and not say a word. And if he asks you in, don't go!"

Mr. Utterson jerked with fright at the butler's strange words, stumbled, and almost fell. For a moment, he could not bring himself to go on. Then he gathered up his courage, took a deep breath, and followed Poole through the laboratory to the office door.

Poole knocked with an uncertain hand. "Mr. Utterson is here and would like to see you, Dr. Jekyll," he called. As he spoke, he motioned with his hands for Mr. Utterson to listen carefully.

A voice spoke from within the office. "Tell him I cannot see anyone," it whined.

"Thank you, sir," Poole answered. He led Mr. Utterson back to the kitchen. There he stopped and looked the lawyer straight in the eyes. "Mr. Utterson, was that my master's voice?" he asked.

"It seems much changed," the lawyer replied nervously. He searched Poole's face for some explanation of the strange goings-on.

"Changed?" repeated the butler. "I should say so! I have worked for Dr. Jekyll for twenty years,

and I think I know the sound of his voice. I tell you, the doctor has been done away with. It happened eight days ago, when we heard him scream. I don't know who is in there now, but he cries out to heaven in a terrible voice! You wouldn't like to hear those cries, Mr. Utterson. They would chill your soul."

"This is a very strange tale," Mr. Utterson said, chewing nervously on his finger. "But suppose you're right. Suppose Dr. Jekyll was murdered. Why would the murderer stay here? It doesn't make any sense."

"You are a hard man to satisfy, but I will do it," Poole told him. "I think he stays because he needs something. All last week, whoever is in that office has been crying night and day for some sort of medicine. He's written instructions on scraps of paper and thrown them out in the hall. Other than those notes, we never hear from him. He doesn't even come out to eat—we leave his meals outside the door, and he smuggles them in when no one is looking. Meanwhile, he sends me to chemists' shops two and three times a day to fetch different medicines for him. But every time I bring the chemicals here, there is another paper ordering me to return them because they are not right. Whatever this drug is, he wants it very badly."

A chemist's shop is what we call a drugstore.

"Do you have any of these notes?" Mr. Utterson asked.

Poole felt around in his pocket and pulled out a crumpled note. He handed it to the lawyer. It read:

Dr. Jekyll sends his best regards to Mr. Maw. He must tell you that the last sample was impure and useless. Some years ago, Dr. Jekyll purchased a large quantity of this chemical from you. I beg you to search with care to find some of that original medicine. If some can be found, forward it to me at once. I will pay anything. I cannot tell you how important it is for me to get some of the old medicine.

Up to then the letter had run calmly enough. But then there was a sudden splutter of the pen, as if Dr. Jekyll could no longer hold back his terror. *For God's sake,* he had scribbled, *find me some of the old!*

"This is a strange note," Mr. Utterson said.

"How do you happen to have it open? Didn't you deliver it as your master asked you to?"

"The man at Maw's was so angry that he threw it back at me as if it were a clod of dirt," Poole explained.

"Are you sure this is written in the doctor's hand?" Mr. Utterson asked.

"I think so," Poole said. "But what difference does that make? I've seen the man who wrote this!"

"You've seen him?" Mr. Utterson repeated, astonished. "How?"

"I came into the laboratory one day and surprised him there. He must have been looking for some of that mysterious medicine, for he was digging around in one of the crates. He looked up when I came in, cried out, and ran back into the office. I only saw him for a moment, but I tell you, the sight made my hair stand on end. Sir, if that was my master, why did he have a mask over his face? If that was my master, why did he cry out like a rat and run away from me?"

"I think I begin to understand what's going on," Mr. Utterson said slowly. "Dr. Jekyll must have one of those diseases that deforms the victim's face. That is why he sounds different, why he wears a mask, why he avoids his friends. And that is why he is so desperate to find the medicine that may cure him. I do so hope he can! It is a sad tale, to be sure, but it is not as horrifying as murder."

"Sir," said the butler, trembling with the strain of his emotions, "that man was *not* my master. Dr. Jekyll is tall and heavyset. The man I saw was small—almost like a dwarf. Do you think I do not know my master after twenty years? No, sir, I don't know what that terrible creature was, but I am certain it was never Dr. Jekyll. I truly believe that there was murder done."

"All right, Poole," the lawyer replied. "As much as I respect the wishes of your master, and even though that note you have seems to prove he is still alive, your words have convinced me that something is wrong. It is my duty to break down the door and make certain."

"Ah, Mr. Utterson, now you're talking!" Poole said with relief. "I will help you. There is an ax here in the kitchen, and you can take the fireplace poker for yourself."

Mr. Utterson picked up the poker and balanced it in his hands. "Do you understand that

we are about to place ourselves in some danger?"
he asked.

"I believe I do, sir," Poole replied.

"Before we go ahead, then, let us tell each
other all we know about this matter. That masked
figure that you saw—do you have any idea who
it was?"

"Do you mean was it Mr. Hyde?" Poole asked,
surprised. "Why yes, I think it was. They were the
same size and had the same quick way of moving.
Besides, who else could have come in by the
laboratory door? You have not forgotten that Mr.
Hyde still has a key." He paused. "That's not all.
Have you ever met Mr. Hyde?"

"Yes, I spoke to him once," Mr. Utterson
replied.

"Then you must know as well as the rest of us
that there was something strange about the man,
something out of a nightmare. I can't put it into
words, except to say that whatever it was, it made
your blood feel cold and thin."

"Yes, I have felt that way," Mr. Utterson said.

"Well, when that masked thing jumped out
of the laboratory like a monkey and ran into the
office, terror went down my spine like ice. Oh, I

know it's not strong enough evidence to hold up in court, but a man knows his feelings. I swear to you, that man was Mr. Hyde!"

"I believe you," Mr. Utterson said. "I knew something evil would come of Dr. Jekyll's connection with that man! Poor Henry Jekyll is dead, and his murderer still lurks in that room." He tightened his grip on the poker. "Let's go."

A cloud passed over the moon, and the room was suddenly quite dark. As the two men walked through the laboratory, the eerie silence was broken by the sound of footsteps walking back and forth, back and forth across the office floor.

"So he walks all day," Poole whispered, "and sometimes all night too. It's an uneasy conscience that keeps a man from his rest and drives him to pace back and forth day and night! Tell me, Mr. Utterson, does that sound like my master's foot?"

Mr. Utterson listened to the steps going up and down, up and down in the quiet of the night. The steps fell lightly and oddly, and they were very different from the heavy tread of Henry Jekyll. Mr. Utterson shook his head. "No, it does not," he said. "Do you ever hear any other sounds from within the room?"

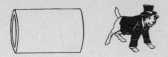

Poole nodded. "Once," he said slowly, "I heard it weeping."

"Weeping?" Mr. Utterson repeated, feeling a sudden chill of horror. "Are you sure?"

"Yes, weeping like a lost soul," said the butler. "I walked away with that sound weighing on my heart, and I felt like weeping myself."

Mr. Utterson did not reply. It was time to act. Poole set down the candle and the two men stepped up to the office door.

"Jekyll," Mr. Utterson shouted, "I demand to see you!" He paused, but there was no answer. "I give you fair warning—we suspect foul play. I *must* see you! If you will not let us in, we will force our way!"

"Utterson!" a voice cried from behind the door. "I beg you, have mercy!"

"That's not Jekyll's voice," cried Mr. Utterson in horror. "It's Hyde's! Break down the door!"

The moment of truth is at hand! What will Mr. Utterson and Poole find on the other side of that door?

11
Death in the Laboratory

At Mr. Utterson's command to break down the door, Poole swung the ax over his shoulder and into the wood. The door shook against the lock and hinges. A horrifying screech of terror rang out from inside the office. Four more times the ax smashed against the door. On the fifth try, the lock finally snapped and the door fell down with a crash.

In the sudden stillness that followed, Mr. Utterson and Poole peered into the office. A fire was glowing in the hearth, and a tea kettle sang on the stove. Papers lay on the worktable. Everything looked completely ordinary—until Mr. Utterson glanced down on the floor.

There was a body there, twisted into an awkward pose and still twitching. Poole and Mr. Utterson hurried forward and carefully rolled the body over onto its back. Mr. Utterson closed his eyes for a moment, filled with dread at what he was about to discover. Then he forced himself to look down at the body. The dead man lying there was none other than Edward Hyde. He was dressed in clothes that were far too big for him—the doctor's clothes. His face moved slightly, as if he was still alive. A glass bottle was clutched in his palm, and the bitter smell of chemicals hung in the air.

"Dear God," Poole whispered, staring down at the dead man. "What has he done?"

"We are too late," Mr. Utterson said sadly. "Mr. Hyde has taken poison and killed himself. There is nothing we can do to him—or for him. All that is left to do is find Dr. Jekyll's body."

Mr. Utterson and Poole searched every inch of the office and the laboratory. They peered into closets, walked into unused rooms, and looked under the stairs, but they could find no trace of Henry Jekyll, dead or alive.

Poole tapped one foot carefully on the floor. "Perhaps he is buried under here," he suggested.

"Or perhaps he fled out the back, through that ugly little door that leads to the side street." Mr. Utterson hurried to that door, but it was locked. The key lay on the floor, twisted and covered with rust.

"This key looks much too rusted to have been used recently," Mr. Utterson commented.

"Used!" Poole exclaimed. "Do you not see, sir, that it is broken? It looks like someone stamped on it."

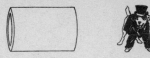

"Yes," Mr. Utterson agreed. "Look, there is even rust along the cracks where the key was broken. It must have been destroyed a long time ago."

The two men looked at each other for a long moment without speaking. Fear was in their hearts and in their eyes.

"This is beyond my understanding," Mr. Utterson said at last. "Let us go back to the office and see if we can find anything else that will help us make sense of all of this."

The two men made their way back into the room. They could not stop themselves from looking nervously at the dead body sprawled in the middle of the floor. Trying to concentrate on their work, they examined the papers on the table, but there was nothing to tell them where Henry Jekyll might be.

Poole pointed to several heaps of white powder in glass dishes, as if the doctor had been about to experiment with them. "That is the same chemical I was always bringing him," the butler said.

Next the men walked up to the hearth. A comfortable chair was pulled close to the fire, and the tea things lay on a table nearby. There was even sugar already in the cup, as if whoever was here had been just about to sit down and have his tea.

Several books lay on a nearby shelf, and one was open on the table. Mr. Utterson saw it was a Bible. Then he peered closely and drew a sharp breath. "Poole, look at this!" he cried, shocked. Scribbled alongside the holy words were horrible curses and drawings of monsters—all done in Dr. Jekyll's hand!

"Why would Dr. Jekyll do such a terrible thing?" Mr. Utterson wondered aloud. "He respected the Bible. He would never dirty and dishonor it like this."

Poole could only shake his head in disbelief.

Mr. Utterson lay the book down quickly, as if he could no longer bear to touch it. He stepped away from the cozy fire and its shocking discovery, and found himself in front of the mirror that stood in the corner. He almost expected some horror to leap out at him from the shadowy glass. Instead, all he saw was a reflection of the room behind him. It was an ordinary sight that gave no clue of the horrible thing that had happened there.

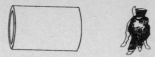

"This mirror has seen some strange things," Poole whispered, coming to stand beside Mr. Utterson.

Mr. Utterson said, "Why would Dr. Jekyll"— he paused, shivering a little at having to speak the name of his dead friend—"want a mirror in his office?"

"A good question," Poole said, but he was unable to give an answer.

Next Mr. Utterson turned to Dr. Jekyll's desk. It was covered with a large number of papers in tidy piles. On top of them all was a large envelope. Mr. Utterson's name was written on it in the doctor's handwriting.

Mr. Utterson unsealed the envelope and pulled out several papers. The first was Dr. Jekyll's will, including the same strange terms about his death and disappearance. But in place of the name of Edward Hyde, the lawyer was surprised and horrified to read his own name. All of Dr. Jekyll's fortune was left not to Mr. Hyde, but to Mr. Utterson!

Mr. Utterson stared at the paper in amazement. Then he looked up at Poole. "My head is dizzy with confusion," the lawyer said.

"Mr. Hyde must have seen this document here and been furious at being written out of the doctor's will. Yet he did not destroy it. I don't understand."

Mr. Utterson looked at the next sheet of paper in the envelope. It was a short note written in Dr. Jekyll's hand and dated that very day. "Poole!" Mr. Utterson cried. "The doctor was alive and here today. Maybe he is not dead after all. Maybe he has only run away. But where, and why? Is he in some other trouble we don't even know about?"

"Why don't you read the note, sir?" Poole suggested.

"Because I am afraid of what it might say," the lawyer admitted. "I pray it contains nothing troubling." With that, he raised the paper to his eyes and read:

My dear Utterson—

When this falls into your hands, I shall have disappeared—in what way I do not know. But my instincts tell me that the end is sure and coming soon. First you must read the letter that Dr. Lanyon told me he would give to you. After you read it, if you care to know more, you may read my enclosed confession.

Your unworthy and unhappy friend,
Henry Jekyll

"Was there another enclosure in the package?" Mr. Utterson asked.

"Yes, sir," Poole said, handing him the last of the documents in the envelope—a fat packet, well sealed.

The lawyer slipped the envelope in his pocket and looked at his watch. "Do not mention this packet to anyone. If your master has fled or died, we may at least be able to save his reputation. It is now ten o'clock. I will go home and read Dr. Lanyon's letter and this document in private. I shall return here before midnight, and then we shall send for the police."

The two men went out of the laboratory, being careful to lock the door behind them, and headed back into the main part of the house. Leaving Poole huddled near the fire with the servants, Mr. Utterson trudged back home to read the letters that would finally explain the mystery.

How can Mr. Utterson be so patient? There's no way I could wait until I got home to read those letters—

I'd rip into them right there! It just goes to show how careful Mr. Utterson is to follow Dr. Jekyll's instructions. As usual, he's putting his own curiosity aside to do exactly what his friend has asked him to do. It won't be long now until all of this story's dark secrets are finally revealed.

12
Dr. Lanyon's Letter

Remember when Mr. Utterson went to visit Dr. Lanyon, only to find him very ill? Dr. Lanyon had received a horrible shock thanks to Dr. Jekyll, and he had refused to talk about his former friend. Three weeks later Dr. Lanyon was dead, but he left Mr. Utterson a letter that was not to be opened until Dr. Jekyll's death or disappearance. Now the time has come to read Dr. Lanyon's letter. This is what he wrote:

To Mr. Utterson:
On January 9, I received a letter from my old friend, Dr. Henry Jekyll. I was very surprised to receive this letter, since I had just seen Henry the night before. I was even more puzzled when I read the letter, for the contents were strange indeed. Dr. Jekyll wrote:

Dear Lanyon,

Even though we have sometimes disagreed on scientific principles, you are one of my oldest and dearest friends. Now I need your help. My life, my honor, and my reason are at your mercy. If you fail me tonight, I am lost.

I need you to cancel any appointments you might have for tonight. Take this letter to my house and go into the office in my laboratory. My butler, Poole, is expecting you. Go to my desk and take out the fourth drawer from the top. It contains a vial, some powders, and a book. If the desk is locked, you must break the lock. Then take the drawer and everything in it back to your house.

At midnight tonight, arrange to be alone in your office. A man will come to your door and say that I have sent him. Give this man the contents of my desk drawer. None of your servants must see this man enter or leave!

After you have done these things, you will have done all I have asked of you and earned my deepest thanks forever. Five minutes later, you will have an explanation if you want it, and then you will understand how important these arrangements are to saving my life and my mind. Please do not fail me! I am working under a black cloud of despair, and even the threat of death. Your help is the only thing that can save me. Serve me well and save your friend.

Henry Jekyll

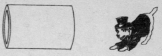

When I read this letter, I was sure my friend had lost his mind. Still, he was once a good friend, and I owed it to him to do what he asked. So I went to Dr. Jekyll's house, where I found Poole waiting for me as promised. It seems he had also received a letter telling him to expect me and to allow me to take the items from Dr. Jekyll's office. I took the particular drawer from Dr. Jekyll's desk, placed it in a bag, and brought it back to my house.

Once I was at home, I could not help but examine the drawer's contents. First I found a container of white powder that looked something like salt. Then I noticed a bottle half full of blood-red liquid with a strong chemical smell. There was also a small book listing a series of dates. One of the early dates was labeled *total failure*, but other dates were followed with exclamation points. The dates covered a period of many years, but stopped abruptly about one year ago. I guessed this was a record of experiments that Dr. Jekyll had performed, but I could make no sense out of any of it.

I could not understand why Dr. Jekyll was so desperate to have a couple of common-looking chemicals and a notebook filled with dates. How could any of these things possibly save the man's life, honor, or reason? And why did Dr. Jekyll's messenger have to come to my house at midnight, in total secrecy? None of this made the slightest bit of sense to me. The more I thought about it, the more I was sure Dr. Jekyll had lost his mind. I decided to be as careful as I could. Since I was not sure what sort of man would be sent on such a strange errand, I loaded my gun and kept it near me in case I should need to defend myself.

Twelve o'clock had barely rung out over London when I heard a gentle knock at my door. I went to answer it and found a small man crouching on the steps.

"Are you sent by Dr. Jekyll?" I asked.

The strange man nodded. I motioned him to follow me into the house, but he would not come until he looked backward into the street. There was a policeman not far away. When my visitor saw him, he jumped nervously and hurried into the house. It was as if he was terrified of being seen.

The man's sneakiness made me wonder about him. Once we were inside, I laid my hand on my gun and took a closer look at him. He was a small

man, with a face that seemed somehow deformed. There was an odd quality to him, as if something had dirtied the very air around him. I could not understand the strong feeling of hatred and disgust I felt. Just looking at him made my stomach turn! I had only just met him and knew nothing about him, so why should I hate him so much? I could not explain my feelings, but I could not change them either.

There was another strange thing about this man—he was wearing well-made clothes of a rich and tasteful material, but they were much too big for him. His pant legs were rolled up to keep from dragging on the ground, the waist of his jacket fell over his thighs, and the collar of his shirt lay around his shoulders. But this ridiculous appearance did not make me want to laugh. Instead it only made me more sure that something was wrong with the man.

"Have you got it?" my strange visitor asked with great excitement. "Have you got it?" He was so impatient that he actually laid a hand on my arm and began to shake me.

I pushed him away, feeling a pang of iciness race through my blood at his touch. "Come, sir, I do not even know you. Sit down, and let us talk for a while, like gentlemen," I said. Even though I was now quite afraid of my visitor, I was determined to act politely and force him to remember his manners.

But my visitor would not sit down. In fact, he was barely able to stand still. "I beg your pardon, Dr. Lanyon," he said, "but Dr. Jekyll sent me here on a mission of great urgency and importance. I believe you have a drawer—" His voice rose hysterically and he seemed to choke on his words.

I could see the man was desperate. "There it is," I told him, pointing at the drawer which was laying on the floor, still in the bag in which I'd carried it home.

The man sprang to it and paused, his hand pressed over his heart. I could hear his teeth grinding against each other, and his face became so pale and drawn that I began to fear the man was having some sort of fit.

"Pull yourself together," I said. "Everything is as Dr. Jekyll instructed."

The man turned to me with a dreadful smile on his face. Then he jerked the drawer out of the

bag. When he saw that all the contents were there, he gasped so with relief that I was quite terrified.

My visitor quickly brought himself under control. "Please, have you got a glass I could use?" he asked.

I handed him a glass and watched as he mixed some of the white powder into the blood-red liquid. The mixture began to fizz and steam, and its color changed from red to purple to a sickly green. My visitor watched all this with a smile spreading across his face.

"Now," he said, turning to face me, "I must drink this mixture. Will you let me take it outside, where you cannot see the result? Or are you so curious that you wish to watch me drink it here? Think hard before you answer. You can choose to remain no wiser than before. Or you can choose to look upon the light of incredible knowledge. What will it be?"

"You speak in riddles," I complained, sounding much calmer than I really felt. "But I have come this far in the mystery of what you are doing. Let me go all the way and see this to the end."

"I am glad to hear that," said the visitor. "You have long held the narrowest of views, never believing the fantastic things that might be possible in medicine and science and denying the facts when they were presented to you. Now you will see the truth!" With that, he drank the potion in one gulp.

I watched in horror as the man staggered back and clutched the table to keep from falling. A terrible cry came from his lips. He stared with wild eyes, gasping for breath through his wide-open mouth. Then, right before my eyes, his body seemed to swell and change. His face turned black and his features melted like wax, becoming the features of another man.

"No! No!" I screamed, raising my arms to block out the terrible sight. When I could bring myself to look, I screamed again, louder this time, for the strange little man who had entered my house was gone. In his place stood the pale, shaking figure of Henry Jekyll.

What he told me in the next hour I cannot bring myself to put on paper. My soul is sickened by what I saw, by what Jekyll has done. My faith in mankind and in medicine has been destroyed, my life shaken to its roots. I can no longer sleep, and terror is my companion day and night. Dr. Jekyll

has shown me something so morally repulsive that
I can no longer bear to live. I cannot even think
about it without frightening myself all over again.
I will say but one thing to you, Utterson, and that

should be more than enough. The creature who came to my house that night was Mr. Hyde. Dr. Jekyll admitted it himself. Yes, Edward Hyde, the murderer of Sir Danvers Carew.

Hastie Lanyon

Wow! So Dr. Jekyll and Mr. Hyde are one and the same person! But why would Dr. Jekyll transform himself into such an evil man? It's time to read Dr. Jekyll's letter to Mr. Utterson.

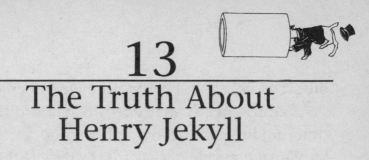

13
The Truth About Henry Jekyll

Mr. Utterson has read Dr. Lanyon's description of what happened that terrible night when he found out Dr. Jekyll and Mr. Hyde were the same person. But there are still a lot of unanswered questions, so Utterson opens the sealed envelope that Dr. Jekyll left him. In this letter, Dr. Jekyll explains everything.

My dear Gabriel—

I was born into a large fortune and enjoyed hard work. I wanted to be respected and well-liked, so there was no reason to think I would not have an honorable and distinguished future. Yet I could not help finding pleasure in acts that would have ruined my reputation completely had people found out about them. Of course I knew that these acts were wrong, but the temptation was too much for me. That is the nature of evil—it disguises itself as something pleasant and inviting, even when it is exactly the opposite. Although I was ashamed of my secret behavior, I could not help but enjoy it.

Because of my evil deeds, I had a difficult time holding my head high in good society. I knew that if people discovered the terrible things I did—and how much I enjoyed doing them—they would no longer have anything to do with me. My reputation and my life would be ruined. I could not live with that fact.

Because of this struggle, I became fascinated with the nature of good and evil. It seemed to me that every person was made up of good and bad, and that these two parts were always fighting against each other. That's how it was with me. I had such high expectations for myself that even the smallest failure made me fall into despair. Yet I could not stop myself from doing horrible things.

I devoted more and more of my studies to this matter and finally came to a startling conclusion— man is not merely one but truly two. I asked myself, what if each part could be split into a separate person? Life would be much simpler then. The evil part could commit his deeds without the worry of ruining his reputation, while the good part could continue his honest work with no fear of the disgrace that might come from his darker half.

I knew some chemicals could cause tremendous changes in people. I began to experiment, searching for a potion that would allow a complete split to occur. I searched for new substances and tried every sort of different mixture. At last, I came up with a mixture that would work. But who could I test it on, except for myself? It was a terrible choice to make. On the one hand, the result could well have been death or madness. But if I failed to try, I would never know if this incredible experiment could succeed.

Madness doesn't mean getting angry. It means losing your mind. Dr. Jekyll was worried that if he drank the potion, he'd go crazy and never be himself again.

In the end, I could not stop myself. Late one awful night, I mixed the chemicals together and watched them boil and smoke. I was filled with a strong glow of courage as I raised the glass to my lips and drank the potion.

The pain and sickness that followed were almost unbearable. My bones ground together and I was tortured by fits of shivering and nausea. But when they faded away, I felt like a new man—younger, lighter, happier. I felt terribly wicked too—ten times more wicked than I had ever dared to be when I was Dr. Jekyll. This knowledge filled me with delight and excitement.

There was no mirror in my laboratory then, although I later brought one in just so I could watch the transformations. But it was very early in the morning, and I knew everyone in my house was asleep. So I crept into my bedroom and got my first look at the man I called Edward Hyde.

He was much smaller and younger than I was. I think that was because the evil side of my nature was not as developed as my good side, so it took up less of myself. But the evil in Mr. Hyde's soul had deformed and decayed his face and body. This did not bother me, however. I looked on the twisted, ugly form and welcomed him as part of my own self.

I have noticed that everyone who comes in contact with Mr. Hyde draws back in horror.

I think this is because all human beings are a mixture of good and evil. But Edward Hyde alone on this earth was pure evil. People recognized this difference at once, even if they could not put it into words.

I lingered only a few moments before the mirror, for the most important part of my experiment still had to be done. I had to see if I had lost my identity completely. A terrible thought struck me—what if I could not change myself back? I would have to live the rest of my life as Edward Hyde! No one would recognize me. I would have no identity, nothing to call my own. Even my own servants would throw me out of the house, and I would have nowhere to go! Quickly, I drank the potion and suffered once more the pain of transformation. But my reward was worth all my suffering, for I found myself changed back into Henry Jekyll.

That night, I came to a crossroads in my life. I had let my good side sleep while the drug released my evil nature. It was not the drug itself that was evil—it was my own desires that caused it to free the darkness inside of me.

Now I could be two people with two very different appearances—the evil Hyde, and the same old Henry Jekyll, whose dull life I was already starting to hate.

Yes, I must confess my life as Henry Jekyll was boring, filled with little but study and work. And although people respected me, I found it harder and harder to pretend to be the upstanding man they believed me to be. After all, they had no knowledge of my evil deeds—my experiments with drugs and the violent crimes I committed and *enjoyed*.

At last I had found a way to escape Henry Jekyll's dullness and longing for respectability. All I had to do was drink my potion and I became Edward Hyde—a man who could do whatever he liked and not really care what people thought of his evil deeds. The whole idea made me laugh.

And so I became a slave to the potion and welcomed Edward Hyde into my life. It was pleasant to feel young again and to have the energy to enjoy a life so different from the one I lived as Dr. Jekyll. After all, no matter what Edward Hyde did, it had nothing to do with Henry Jekyll.

I set up a whole life for Edward Hyde. I furnished an apartment in Soho for him and told my servants that Mr. Hyde was to have full run of my house. Then an act of cruelty against a child caused the anger of a man passing by—a man I later came to learn was your friend. My actions that night drew a furious crowd, and there were moments when I feared for my life. To calm them, Edward Hyde had to bring them to the door and pay them with a check drawn in the name of Henry Jekyll. I feared such a thing might happen again, but I soon thought of a way to avoid that. All I had to do was open a bank account in Edward Hyde's name and disguise my handwriting to invent a signature for him. I had even written Mr. Hyde into my will so that if anything ever happened to Henry Jekyll, I could still enjoy life as Edward Hyde.

But in time, Edward Hyde began to frighten me. The things he did went from unpleasant to truly monstrous. He was capable of such heartless cruelty that I could scarcely believe he was really a part of me. Hyde thought nothing of stealing from innocent people or of committing violence against them. Of course, the law would say that

Mr. Hyde was the only one guilty of these crimes. I, Dr. Jekyll was not touched by them in any way. Even my conscience found a way to sleep in peace while Mr. Hyde did his evil deeds.

About two months before the murder of Sir Danvers Carew, I went to sleep as Henry Jekyll. When I woke in the morning, I felt different— strange, not at all like myself. I looked all around me. Something inside me kept whispering, *You are not where you should be.* This idea seemed so silly that I had to smile. Then my eyes fell on my hand, lying on the pillow. The hand was not mine. My hand was large, firm, white, and well-formed. But the hand I saw now in the yellow light of a London morning, lying half-shut on the blankets, was darker, thinner, and covered with thick black hair. It was the hand of Edward Hyde!

I must have stared at that hand for a full minute before terror woke within me, as sudden and as startling as a clash of cymbals. I leaped from my bed and rushed to the mirror. What I saw there turned my blood to ice. I had gone to bed as Henry Jekyll, but I had awakened as Edward Hyde!

How could this be explained? I asked myself.

Then I thought of an even more important question: *How could it be fixed?* It was late in the morning, and the servants were up and about. But the potion was in the cabinet of my laboratory office, a long walk down two flights of stairs and a hallway from where I now stood, shaking in horror. I could cover my face as I traveled there, but what was the use of that when anyone could see the change in the size of my body?

Suddenly I saw the answer to my problem, and I was filled with an incredible sense of relief. I realized that my servants were already used to seeing Mr. Hyde coming and going. And so I dressed as well as I could in clothes that did not fit me, and hurried through the house. One of the servants drew back at seeing Mr. Hyde at such an hour, and dressed so ridiculously, but he said nothing. Ten minutes later, I had returned to my own shape as Henry Jekyll. I was sitting down to a breakfast I had no appetite for.

This experience frightened me badly. Edward Hyde had more power over me than I had ever expected. He was taking over, and Henry Jekyll might be lost forever.

I knew I had to choose between my two selves. To choose Jekyll meant that I would have to deny the pleasures I had so come to enjoy. But to choose Hyde meant to be hated and friendless for the rest of my days. In the end, I could not give up my good name and comfortable life. I chose to remain as Henry Jekyll.

For two months, I remained true to my intentions and led an upstanding life. But as time passed, I forgot how frightened I had been that morning I woke up as Hyde. Soon I became tortured with the longing to become Edward Hyde again. It was as if Hyde was trapped inside me, screaming to be free.

Finally I could take no more. I drank the potion, and Hyde came out roaring. He had been caged up for so long that now there was no controlling him.

That night, in the form of Mr. Hyde, I met Sir Danvers Carew on the street. I was so wild, so eager to run free and commit my dark deeds, that I could not bear to listen to the gentleman's pleasant, unimportant words. I struck him.

As Sir Carew fell to the ground, I was filled with a dreadful glee. Every blow to that poor body filled me with joy. I kept on and on, until I was completely exhausted. Then a thrill of terror went straight through my heart. It was as if a fog had lifted. At that moment, I, Henry Jekyll felt the pain of every evil deed Edward Hyde had ever done.

I returned to my room and drank the potion that restored me to Henry Jekyll. Then I fell to my knees and cried. I saw my whole life before me, from the days of my childhood to those as a doctor and a scientist. Again and again, these happy visions were blotted out by the horrors of the murder I had committed that night. I begged God to forgive me.

Finally I saw the answer, and my grief was changed to joy. I knew that to live as Hyde was impossible. From now on, I would be Henry Jekyll, and Henry Jekyll alone. How happy I was to return to a life filled with rules and respectability! How I rejoiced as I locked the laboratory's back door—the door Hyde had used to come and go—and ground the key under my heel until it broke!

The next day I heard the news that the murder had been witnessed by a maidservant, the victim was an important man, and the whole world knew that Mr. Hyde was the killer. I think I was glad to know that returning to the shape of Mr. Hyde meant I would be hung for murder. As Dr. Jekyll I was safe, but if I let Mr. Hyde peep out for just an instant, the hands of all men would be raised against him.

After that, I swore to live a kind, good, generous life. The days that followed were sweet. I worked to relieve suffering and found great joy in the help I gave to others. But I was a fool to think these quiet, happy days could last forever.

As time passed, the temptation to release Mr. Hyde came over me again. I grew impatient with the order of my life, and the darkness inside me began to growl for release like a dog on a chain. Of course I had no intention of bringing Mr. Hyde back to life—the mere idea terrified me.

One fine, clear January day, the evil inside me finally rose to take over all of my soul. I was sitting in the park, lazily enjoying the sounds of the birds. I felt good about myself, especially when I thought of how many good deeds I had done—more than many men bothered to do. Just as I was enjoying those self-centered thoughts, I was filled with a horrible sickness. I shuddered and almost fainted. When I came to myself again,

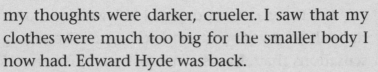

my thoughts were darker, crueler. I saw that my clothes were much too big for the smaller body I now had. Edward Hyde was back.

What could I do? Just moments ago I was a wealthy man, worthy of respect. Now I was a known murderer, hunted by the police. I could not be seen in public in the form of Edward Hyde! Yet the drugs that would change me back to Dr. Jekyll were at home, far away.

Suddenly, I thought of my old friend, Dr. Lanyon. Would he help me? It was my only hope.

I fled to a nearby hotel and took a room. There I used Dr. Jekyll's handwriting to compose a letter to Dr. Lanyon, begging his help. I also wrote a letter to Poole, telling him to allow Dr. Lanyon to take items from my desk. I sent the letters out, then waited in the room until midnight, filled with fear and hatred.

Everything went as I planned. I made my way to Dr. Lanyon's house, where I drank the potion and was returned to the form of Dr. Jekyll. I knew that what Dr. Lanyon saw that night had a terrible effect on him, but the whole episode was like a dream to me. I went home and fell into a deep, peaceful sleep.

But the very next day, as I was walking down the hall to my laboratory, I felt again the raging sensations that always came just seconds before I changed into Mr. Hyde. That time, it took a double dose of the powder to restore me to myself. Six hours later, the terrible transformation happened again. I realized that Hyde was taking control. The fear of hanging for my crime should Hyde be discovered no longer bothered me. Now the only thing I feared was Hyde himself.

From that day forward, it was only by taking great amounts of the drug that I could be Henry Jekyll, and my time in Jekyll's body lasted just a little while. Day or night, waking or sleeping, the second I let my guard down I became Edward Hyde. My true self was a prisoner to that evil creature.

The stronger Hyde grew, the weaker Jekyll became. My body boiled with terror and hatred and a raging energy for life. It was like being an animal—there was nothing human in Hyde now. He needed Jekyll to survive, for if Hyde were seen in his own form, he would be arrested and hanged. Only in the form of Dr. Jekyll was he safe.

I began to rely more and more on the medicine. But the original supply of the salt I used had run low, and fresh supplies did not work the same way. Poole will tell you that I sent him to every chemist's shop in London, all in vain. I now think that my first supply of the salt was impure. It was that unknown impurity that made the potion work.

As I write this, I have used up the last of that original salt. This is the last time that I will see Henry Jekyll's face—my own face—in the mirror. I must finish this before the drug wears off and Edward Hyde returns—forever.

What will happen to me when I become Edward Hyde? Will I remain trapped in this room, unable to show my face outside? Will I be captured and hung for the murder of Sir Danvers Carew? It doesn't matter. This moment is the true hour of my death. What follows concerns Edward Hyde, not myself.

So here I lay down my pen and seal up this confession. The sad life of Henry Jekyll is at its end.

Mr. Utterson finished the letter and laid it down with a shaking hand. Tears ran down his face as he wept for his dead friend and the terrible torments he had suffered.

"If only Henry had asked for help!" he said to himself. "If he had come to me when all this trouble began, I would have done my best to help him. Poor Henry. What a pity that Henry was so worried about saving his reputation that he had to hide his sins from me—and even from himself."

With these thoughts in mind, Mr. Utterson headed out the door and back to Dr. Jekyll's house. It was time to talk to Poole and fill him in on all that had happened. He saw no need to tell the truth of this evening's events to the police. It would be enough to tell them that Hyde had apparently killed Dr. Jekyll, then killed himself. The lie would at least save Dr. Jekyll's reputation. It was the last act Mr. Utterson could do for his dear, dead friend.

And so at last the puzzle of Dr. Jekyll and Mr. Hyde is solved! This is one of my favorite mystery stories. Throughout the book, Robert Louis Stevenson gave us strange clues about the relationship between the good Henry Jekyll and the evil Edward Hyde. Remember Dr. Jekyll's will? And what about the mysterious cane? Or that unusual conversation that Mr. Utterson had with Dr. Lanyon just before the good doctor died?

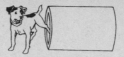

We knew there was something strange about Jekyll and Hyde, but it remained a mystery until the exciting conclusion.

Whew! All these clues are making this little dog hungry! I'm calling my next adventure, "The Strange Case of Wishbone and the Missing Tuna Sandwich." See ya!

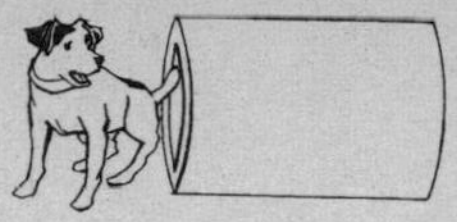